Alfred B. Douglas

The City of the Soul

Alfred B. Douglas

The City of the Soul

ISBN/EAN: 9783337406110

Printed in Europe, USA, Canada, Australia, Japan

Cover: Foto ©Andreas Hilbeck / pixelio.de

More available books at **www.hansebooks.com**

THE CITY OF THE SOUL

THE

CITY OF THE SOUL

LONDON

GRANT RICHARDS

9 HENRIETTA STREET, COVENT GARDEN, W.C.

1899

CONTENTS

THE CITY OF THE SOUL

CONTENTS

THE CITY OF THE SOUL

THE CITY OF THE SOUL

In the salt terror of a stormy sea
There are high attitudes the mind forgets;
And undesired days are hunting nets
To snare the souls that fly Eternity.
But we being gods will never bend the knee,
Though sad moons shadow every sun that sets,
And tears of sorrow be like rivulets
To feed the shallows of Humility.

Within my soul are some mean gardens found
Where drooped flowers are, and unsung melodies,
And all companioning of piteous things.
But in the midst is one high terraced ground,
Where level lawns sweep through the stately trees
And the great peacocks walk like painted kings.

2

THE CITY OF THE SOUL

What shall we do, my soul, to please the King?
Seeing he hath no pleasure in the dance,
And hath condemned the honeyed utterance
Of silver flutes and mouths made round to sing.
Along the wall red roses climb and cling,
And oh! my prince, lift up thy countenance,
For there be thoughts like roses that entrance
More than the languors of soft lute-playing.

Think how the hidden things that poets see
In amber eves or mornings crystalline,
Hide in the soul their constant quenchless light,
Till, called by some celestial alchemy,
Out of forgotten depths, they rise and shine
Like buried treasure on Midsummer night.

THE CITY OF THE SOUL

The fields of Phantasy are all too wide,
My soul runs through them like an untamed thing.
It leaps the brooks like threads, and skirts the
   ring
Where fairies danced, and tenderer flowers hide.
The voice of music has become the bride
Of an imprisoned bird with broken wing.
What shall we do, my soul, to please the King,
We that are free, with ample wings untied?

We cannot wander through the empty fields
Till beauty like a hunter hurl the lance.
There are no silver snares and springes set,
Nor any meadow where the plain ground yields.
O let us then with ordered utterance,
Forge the gold chain and twine the silken net.

THE CITY OF THE SOUL

Each new hour's passage is the acolyte
Of inarticulate song and syllable,
And every passing moment is a bell,
To mourn the death of undiscerned delight.
Where is the sun that made the noon-day bright,
And where the midnight moon?   O let us tell,
In long carved line and painted parable,
How the white road curves down into the night.

Only to build one crystal barrier
Against this sea which beats upon our days;
To ransom one lost moment with a rhyme!
Or if fate cries and grudging gods demur,
To clutch Life's hair, and thrust one naked phrase
Like a lean knife between the ribs of Time.

5

THE BALLAD OF SAINT VITUS

Vitus came tripping over the grass
When all the leaves in the trees were green,
Through the green meadows he did pass
On the day he was full seventeen.

The lark was singing up over his head,
As he went by so lithe and fleet,
And the flowers danced in white and red
At the treading of his nimble feet.

His neck was as brown as the brown earth is
When first the young brown plough-boys delve it,

THE BALLAD OF SAINT VITUS

And his lips were as red as mulberries
And his eyes were like the soft black velvet.

His silk brown hair was touched with bronze,
And his brown cheeks had the tender hue
That like a dress the brown earth dons
When the pink carnations bloom anew.

He was slim as the reeds that sway all along
The banks of the lake, and as straight as a rush,
And as he passed he sang a song,
And his voice was as sweet as the voice of a
    thrush.

He sang of the Gardens of Paradise,
And the light of God that never grows dim,
And the Cherubim with their radiant eyes,
And the rainbow wings of the Seraphim.

THE BALLAD OF SAINT VITUS

And the host as countless as all days,
That worships there, and ceases not,
Singing and praising God always,
With lute and flute and angelot.

And the blessèd light of Mary's face
As she sits among these pleasant sounds,
And Christ that is the Prince of Grace,
And the five red flowers that be His wounds.

And so he went till he came to the doors
Of the ivory house of his father the King,
And all through the golden corridors,
As he passed along, he ceased to sing.

But a pagan priest had seen him pass,
And heard his voice as he went along
Through the fields of the bending grass,
And he heard the words of the holy song.

THE BALLAD OF SAINT VITUS

And he sought the King where he sat on his throne,
And the tears of wrath were in his eyes,
And he said, " O Sire, be it known
That thy son singeth in this wise :

" Of the blessed light of Mary's face
As she sits amidst sweet pleasant sounds,
And how that Christ is the Prince of Grace,
And hath five flowers that be His wounds."

And when the King had heard this thing,
His brow grew black as a winter night,
And he bade the pages seek and bring
Straightway the prince before his sight.

And Vitus came before the King,
And the King cried out, " I pray thee, Son,
Sing now the song that thou didst sing
When thou cam'st through the fields anon."

9

THE BALLAD OF SAINT VITUS

And the face of the prince grew white as milk,
And he answered nought, but under the band
That held his doublet of purple silk
Round his slight waist, he thrust his hand.

And the King picked up a spear, and cried,
" What hast thou there ? by the waters of Styx,
Speak or I strike," and the boy replied,
" Sweet Sire, it is a crucifix."

And the King grew black with rage and grief,
And for full a moment he spake no word.
And the spear in his right hand shook like a leaf,
And the vein on his brow was a tight blue cord.

Then he laughed and said, in bitter scorn,
" Take me this Christian fool from my sight,
Lock him in the turret till the morn,
And let him dance alone to-night.

THE BALLAD OF SAINT VITUS

" He shall sit in the dark while the courtly ball

All the gay night sweeps up and down

On the polished floor of the golden hall,

And thus shall he win his martyr's crown."

Thus spake the King, and the courtiers smiled,

And Vitus hung his head for shame;

And he thought, "I am punished like a child,

That would have died for Christ's dear Name."

And so 'twas done, and on that night,

While silk and sword, with fan and flower,

Danced in the hall in the golden light,

Prince Vitus sat in the lone dark tower.

But the King bethought him, and was moved,

Ere the short summer night was done,

And his heart's blood yearned for the son he loved,

His dainty prince, his only son.

And all alone he climbed the stair,
With the tired feet of a tired King,
And came to the door, and lo! he was 'ware
Of the sound of flute and lute-playing.

And as the King stood there amazed,
The iron door flew open wide,
And the King fell down on his knees as he gazed
At the wondrous thing he saw inside.

For the room was filled with a soft sweet light
Of ambergris and apricot,
And round the walls were angels bright,
With lute and flute and angelot.

On lute and angelot they played,
With their gold heads bowed upon the strings,
And the soft wind that the slim flutes made,
Stirred in the feathers of their wings.

THE BALLAD OF SAINT VITUS

And in the midst serene and sweet,
With God's light on his countenance,
Was Vitus, with his gold shod feet,
Dancing in a courtly dance.

And round him were archangels four,
Michael, who guards God's citadel,
Raphael, whom children still implore,
And Gabriel and Uriel.

Thus long ago was Christ's behest,
And the saving grace that His red wounds be,
Unto this king made manifest,
And all his land of Sicily.

God sits within the highest Heaven,
His mercy neither tires nor faints,
All good gifts that may be given,
He gives unto His holy Saints.

THE BALLAD OF SAINT VITUS

This was the joy that Vitus gat;

To dance with Angels knee by knee,

Before he came to man's estate :

God send us all such Company.

                            Amen.

THE TRAVELLING COMPANION

INTO the silence of the empty night
I went, and took my scornèd heart with me,
And all the thousand eyes of heaven were bright;
But Sorrow came and led me back to thee.

I turned my weary eyes towards the sun,
Out of the leaden East like smoke came he.
I laughed and said, " The night is past and done ";
But Sorrow came and led me back to thee.

THE TRAVELLING COMPANION

I turned my face towards the rising moon,
Out of the south she came most sweet to see,
She smiled upon my eyes that loathed the noon;
But Sorrow came and led me back to thee.

I bent my eyes upon the summer land,
And all the painted fields were ripe for me,
And every flower nodded to my hand;
But Sorrow came and led me back to thee.

O Love! O Sorrow! O desired Despair!
I turn my feet towards the boundless sea,
Into the dark I go and heed not where,
So that I come again at last to thee.

A TRIAD OF THE MOON

.

A TRIAD OF THE MOON

LAST night my window played with one moon-
   beam,
And I lay watching till sleep came, and stole
Over my eyelids, and she brought a shoal
Of hurrying thoughts that were her troubled team,
And in the weary ending of a dream
I found this word upon a candid scroll:
" The nightingale is like a poet's soul,
She finds fierce pain in miseries that seem."

Ah me, methought, that she should so devise!
To seek for pain and sing such doleful bars,
That the wood aches and simple flowers cry,
And sea-green tears drench mortal lovers' eyes
She that is made the lure of those young stars
That hang like golden spiders in the sky.

A TRIAD OF THE MOON

II

That she should so devise, to find such lore
Of sighful song and piteous psalmody,
While Joy runs on through summer greenery,
And all Delight is like an open door.
Must then her liquid notes for evermore
Repeat the colour of sad things, and be
Distilled like cassia drops of agony,
From the slow anguish of a heart's bruised core?

Nay, she weeps not because she knows sad songs,
But sings because she weeps; for wilful food
Of her sad singing, she will still decoy
The sweetness that to happy things belongs.
All night with artful woe she holds the wood,
And all the summer day with natural joy.

A TRIAD OF THE MOON

III

My soul is like a silent nightingale
Devising sorrow in a summer night.
Closed eyes in blazing noon put out the light,
And Hell lies in the thickness of a veil.
In every voiceless moment sleeps a wail,
And all the lonely darknesses are bright,
And every dawning of the day is white
With shapes of sorrow fugitive and frail.

My soul is like a flower whose honey-bees
Are pains that sting and suck the sweets untold,
My soul is like an instrument of strings;
I must stretch these to capture harmonies,
And to find songs like buried dust of gold,
Delve with the nightingale for sorrowful things.

SONNET ON THE SONNET

To see the moment holds a madrigal,
To find some cloistered place, some hermitage
For free devices, some deliberate cage
Wherein to keep wild thoughts like birds in thrall ;
To eat sweet honey and to taste black gall,
To fight with form, to wrestle and to rage,
Till at the last upon the conquered page
The shadows of created Beauty fall.

This is the sonnet, this is all delight
Of every flower that blows in every Spring,
And all desire of every desert place ;
This is the joy that fills a cloudy night
When, bursting from her misty following,
A perfect moon wins to an empty space.

21

THE LEGEND OF SPINELLO OF AREZZO

Spinello of Arezzo long ago,
A cunning painter, made a large design
To grace the choir of St. Angelo.
Therein he pictured the exploits divine
Of the Archangel Michael, beautiful
Exceedingly, in wrath most terrible,
Until at last that holy place was full
Of warring angels; and that one who fell
From the high places of the highest Heaven
Into the deep abyss of lowest Hell,

THE LEGEND OF SPINELLO OF AREZZO

He pictured too, in mad disaster driven
Before the conquering hosts of Paradise.
And him the painter drew in uncouth shape,
A foul misshapen monster with fierce eyes,
Of hideous form, half demon and half ape.

And lo! it fell out as he slept one night,
His soul, in the sad neutral land of dreams
That lies between the darkness and the light,
Was 'ware of one whose eyes were soft as beams
Of summer moonlight, and withal as sad.
Dark was his colour, and as black his hair
As hyacinths by night, his sweet lips had
A curve as piteous as sweet lovers wear
When they have lost their loves; so fair was he
So melancholy, yet withal so proud,
He seemed a prince whose woes might move a
    tree

To find a tearful voice and weep aloud.

He spoke, his voice was tunable and mellow,

But soft as are the western winds that stir

The summer leaves, and thus he said, "Spinello,

Why dost thou wrong me? I am Lucifer."

SPRING

Wake up again, sad heart, wake up again!
(I heard the birds this morning singing sweet.)
Wake up again!   The sky was crystal clear,
      And washed quite clean with rain;
And far below my heart stirred with the year,
Stirred with the year and sighed . O pallid feet
Move now at last, O heart that sleeps with pain .
      Rise up and hear
The voices in the valleys, run to meet
The songs and shadows.   O wake up again!

25

SPRING

Put out green leaves, dead tree, put out green
    leaves!
(Last night the moon was soft and kissed the air.)
Put out green leaves! The moon was in the skies,
    All night she wakes and weaves.
The dew was on the grass like fairies' eyes,
Like fairies' eyes. O tree so black and bare,
Remember all the fruits the full gold sheaves;
    For nothing dies,
The songs that are, are silences that were,
Summer was Winter. O put out green leaves!

Break through the earth, pale flower, break through
    the earth!
(All day the lark has sung a madrigal.)
Break through the earth that lies not lightly yet
    And waits thy patient birth,
Waits for the jonquil and the violet,

SPRING

The violet.   Full soon the heavy pall

Will be a bed, and in the noon of mirth

      Some rivulet

Will bubble in my wilderness, some call

Will touch my silence.   O break through the earth

ENNUI

Alas! and oh that Spring should come again
Upon the soft wings of desired days,
And bring with her no anodyne to pain,
And no discernment of untroubled ways.
There was a time when her yet distant feet,
Guessed by some prescience more than half divine,
Gave to my listening ear such happy warning,
     That fresh, serene, and sweet,
My thoughts soared up like larks into the morning,
From the dew-sprinkled meadows crystalline.

Soared up into the heights celestial,
And saw the whole world like a ball of fire,
Fashioned to be a monster playing ball

ENNUI

For the enchantment of my young desire.
And yesterday they flew to this black cloud,
(Missing the way to those ethereal spheres.)
And saw the earth a vision of affright,

    And men a sordid crowd,

And felt the fears and drank the bitter tears,
And saw the empty houses of Delight.

The sun has sunk into a moonless sea,
And every road leads down from Heaven to Hell,
The pearls are numbered on youth's rosary,
I have outlived the days desirable.
What is there left?   And how shall dead men sing
Unto the loosened strings of Love and Hate,
Or take strong hands to Beauty's ravishment?

    Who shall devise this thing,

To give high utterance to Miscontent,
Or make Indifference articulate?

WINE OF SUMMER

THE sun holds all the earth and all the sky
From the gold throne of this midsummer day.
In the soft air the shadow of a sigh
Breathes on the leaves and scarcely makes them
   sway.
The wood lies silent in the shimmering heat,
Save where the insects make a lazy drone,
And ever and anon from some tree near,
     A dove's enamoured moan,
Or distant rook's faint cawing harsh and sweet,
Comes dimly floating to my listening ear.

WINE OF SUMMER

Right in the wood's deep heart I lay me down,
And look up at the sky between the leaves,
Through delicate lace I see her deep blue gown.
Across a fern a scarlet spider weaves
From branch to branch a slender silver thread,
And hangs there shining in the white sunbeams,
A ruby tremulous on a streak of light.
                And high above my head
One spray of honeysuckle sways and dreams,
With one wild honey-bee for acolyte.

My nest is all untrod and virginal,
And virginal the path that led me here,
For all along the grass grew straight and tall,
And live things rustled in the thicket near:
And briar rose stretched out to sweet briar rose
Wild slender arms, and barred the way to me
With many a flowering arch, rose-pink or white,

WINE OF SUMMER

As bending carefully,
Leaving unbroken all their blossoming bows,
I passed along, a reverent neophyte.

The air is full of soft imaginings,
They float unseen beneath the hot sunbeams,
Like tired moths on heavy velvet wings.
They droop above my drowsy head like dreams.
The hum of bees, the murmuring of doves,
The soft faint whispering of unnumbered trees,
Mingle with unreal things, and low and deep
From visionary groves,
Imagined lutes make voiceless harmonies,
And false flutes sigh before the gates of sleep.

O rare sweet hour!   O cup of golden wine!
The night of these my days is dull and dense,
And stars are few, be this the anodyne!

32

WINE OF SUMMER

Of many woes the perfect recompense.
I thought that I had lost for evermore
The sense of this ethereal drunkenness,
This fierce desire to live, to breathe, to be;
  But even now, no less
Than in the merry noon that danced before
My tedious night, I taste its ecstasy.

Taste, and remember all the summer days
That lie, like gold reflections in the lake
Of vanished years, unreal but sweet always;
Soft luminous shadows that I may not take
Into my hands again, but still discern
Drifting like gilded ghosts before my eyes,
Beneath the waters of forgotten things,
  Sweet with faint memories,
And mellow with old loves that used to burn
Dead summer days ago, like fierce red kings.

D

WINE OF SUMMER

And this hour too must die, even now the sun
Droops to the sea, and with untroubled feet
The quiet evening comes: the day is done.
The air that throbbed beneath the passionate
    heat
Grows calm and cool and virginal again.
The colour fades and sinks to sombre tones,
As when in youthful cheeks a blush grows dim.
        Hushed are the monotones
Of doves and bees, and the long flowery lane
Rustles beneath the wind in playful whim.

Gone are the passion and the pulse that beat
With fevered strokes, and gone the unseen things
That clothed the hour with shining raiment meet
To deck enchantments and imaginings.
No joy is here but only neutral peace
And loveless languor and indifference,

34

WINE OF SUMMER

And faint remembrance of lost ecstasy.

The darkening shades increase,

My dreams go out like tapers—I must hence.

Far off I hear Night calling to the sea.

ODE TO AUTUMN

Thou sombre lady of down-bended head,
And weary lashes drooping to the cheek,
With sweet sad fold of lips uncomforted,
And listless hands more tired with strife than meek;
Turn here thy soft brown feet, and to my heart,
Unmatched to Summer's golden minstrelsy,
Or Spring's shrill pipe of joy, sing once again
    Sad songs, and I to thee
Well tuned, will answer that according part
That jarred with those young seasons' gladder
    strain.

ODE TO AUTUMN

Give me thy empty branches for the biers
Of perished joys, thy winds to sigh my sighs,
Thy falling leaves to count my falling tears,
And all thy mists to dim my aching eyes.
There is no comfort in thy lips, and none
In thy cold arms, nor pity in thy breast,
But better 'tis in gray hours to have grief,
      Than to affront the sun
With sunless woe, when every flower and leaf
Conspires to make the season merriest.

The drip of rain-drops on the sodden earth,
The trampled mud-stained grass, the shifting
     leaves,
The silent hurrying birds, the sickly birth
Of the red sun in misty skies; the sheaves
Of rotting ruined corn, the sudden gusts
Of angry winds, the clouds that fly all night

ODE TO AUTUMN

Before the stormy moon, thy desolate moans,

    All thy decays and rusts,

Thy deaths and dirges, these are tuned aright

To my unquiet soul that sorrow owns.

But ah! thy gentler mood, the honeyed kiss

Of thy faint watery sunshine, thy pale gold,

Thy dark red berries, and the ambergris

That paints the lingering leaves, while on the
    mould,

Their dead make bronze and sepia carpetings

That lightly rustle in thy quiet breath.

These are the shadows of departed smiles,

    The ghosts of happy things;

These break again the broken heart, the whiles

Thou goest on to winter, I to Death.

TWO TRANSLATIONS FROM BAUDELAIRE

HARMONIE DU SOIR

Voici venir le temps

Now is the hour when, swinging in the breeze,
Each flower, like a censer, sheds its sweet.
The air is full of scents and melodies,
O languorous waltz! O swoon of dancing feet!

Each flower, like a censer, sheds its sweet,
The violins are like sad souls that cry,
O languorous waltz! O swoon of dancing feet!
A shrine of Death and Beauty is the sky.

39

The violins are like sad souls that cry,

Poor souls that hate the vast black night of Death;

A shrine of Death and Beauty is the sky.

Drowned in red blood, the Sun gives up his breath.

This soul that hates the vast black night of Death

Takes all the luminous past back tenderly.

Drowned in red blood, the Sun gives up his breath.

Thine image like a monstrance shines in me.

LE BALCON

Mère des souvenirs, mâitresse des mâitresses

MOTHER of Memories!   O mistress-queen!
Oh! all my joy and all my duty thou!
The beauty of caresses that have been,
The evenings and the hearth remember now,
Mother of Memories!   O mistress-queen!

The evenings burning with the glowing fire,
And on the balcony, the rose-stained nights!
How sweet, how kind you were, my soul's desire.   ·
We said things wonderful as chrysolites,
When evening burned beside the glowing fire.

41

How fair the Sun is in the evening!
How strong the soul, how high the heaven's tower '
O first and last of every worshipped thing,
Your odorous heart's-blood filled me like a flower.
How fair the sun is in the evening!

The night grew deep between us like a pall,
And in the dark I guessed your shining eyes,
And drank your breath, O sweet, O honey-gall!
Your little feet slept on me sister-wise.
The night grew deep between us like a pall.

I can call back the days desirable,
And live all bliss again between your knees,
For where else can I find that magic spell
Save in your heart and in your Mysteries.
I can call back the days desirable.

TWO TRANSLATIONS FROM BAUDELAIRE

These vows, these scents, these kisses infinite,

Will they like young suns climbing up the skies,

Rise up from some unfathomable pit,

Washed in the sea from all impurities?

O vows, O scents, O kisses infinite!

PERKIN WARBECK

I

At Turney in Flanders I was born
  Fore-doomed to splendour and sorrow,
For I was a king when they cut the corn,
  And they strangle me to-morrow.

II

Oh! why was I made so red and white,
  So fair and straight and tall?
And why were my eyes so blue and bright,
  And my hands so white and small?

PERKIN WARBECK

III

And why was my hair like the yellow silk,
 And curled like the hair of a king?
And my body like the soft new milk
 That the maids bring from milking?

IV

I was nothing but a weaver's son,
 I was born in a weaver's bed;
My brothers toiled and my sisters spun,
 And my mother wove for our bread.

V

I was the latest child she had,
 And my mother loved me the best.
She would laugh for joy and anon be sad
 That I was not as the rest.

VI

For my brothers and sisters were black as the
    gate
  Whereby I shall pass to-morrow,
But I was white and delicate,
  And born to splendour and sorrow.

VII

And my father the weaver died full soon,
  But my mother lived for me;
And I had silk doublets and satin shoon
  And was nurtured tenderly.

VIII

And the good priests had much joy of me,
  For I had wisdom and wit;
And there was no tongue or subtlety
  But I could master it.

PERKIN WARBECK

IX

And when I was fourteen summers old
　There came an English knight,
With purple cloak and spurs of gold,
　And sword of chrysolite.

X

He rode through the town both sad and slow,
　And his hands lay in his lap;
He wore a scarf as white as the snow,
　And a snow-white rose in his cap.

XI

And he passed me by in the market-place,
　And he reined his horse and stared,
And I looked him fair and full in the face,
　And he stayed with his head all bared.

XII

And he leaped down quick and bowed his knee,
  And took hold on my hand ;
And he said, " Is it ghost or wraith that I see,
  Or the White Rose of England ? "

XIII

And I answered him in the Flemish tongue,
  " My name is Peter Warbeckke,
From Katherine de Faro I am sprung
  And my father was John Osbeckke.

XIV

" My father toiled and weaved with his hand
  And bare neither sword nor shield,
And the White Rose of fair England
  Turned red on Bosworth field."

48

XV

And he answered, "What matter for anything?
   For God hath given to thee
The voice of the king and the face of the king,
   And the king thou shalt surely be."

XVI

And he wrought on me till the vesper bell,
   And I rode forth out of the town:
And I might not bid my mother farewell,
   Lest her.love should seem more than a crown.

XVII

And the sun went down, and the night waxed
   black,
   And the wind sang wearily;
And I thought on my mother, and was fain to go
   back,
   But he would not suffer me.

E

XVIII

And we rode, and we rode, was it nine days or
    three?
  Till we heard the bells that ring
For "my cousin Margaret of Burgundy,"
  And I was indeed a king.

XIX

For I had a hundred fighting-men
  To come at my beck and call,
And I had silk and fine linen
  To line my bed withal.

XX

They dressed me all in silken dresses,
  And little I wot did they reck
Of the precious scents for my golden tresses,
  And the golden chains for my neck.

PERKIN WARBECK

XXI

And all the path for " the rose " to walk
  Was strewn with flowers and posies,
I was the milk-white rose of York,
  The rose of all the roses.

XXII

And the Lady Margaret taught me well,
  Till I spake without lisping
Of Warwick and Clarence and Isabel,
  And " my father " Edward the King.

XXIII

And I sailed to Ireland and to France,
  And I sailed to fair Scotland,
And had much honour and pleasaunce,
  And Katherine Gordon's hand.

51

XXIV

And after that what brooks it to say
    Whither I went or why?
I was as loathe to leave my play
    And fight, as now to die.

XXV

For I was not made for wars and strife
    And blood and slaughtering,
I was but a boy that loved his life,
    And I had not the heart of a king.

XXVI

Oh! why hath God dealt so hardly with me,
    That such a thing should be done,
That a boy should be born with a king's body
    And the heart of a weaver's son?

PERKIN WARBECK

XXVII

I was well pleased to be at the court,
  Lord of the thing that seems;
It was merry to be a prince for sport,
  A king in a kingdom of dreams.

XXVIII

But ever they said I must strive and fight
  To wrest away the crown,
So I came to England in the night
  And I warred on Exeter town.

XXIX

And the King came up with a mighty host
  And what could I do but fly?
I had three thousand men at the most,
  And I was most loath to die.

PERKIN WARBECK.

XXX

And they took me and brought me to London
    town,
    And I stood where all men might see;
I, that had wellnigh worn a crown,
    In a shameful pillory!

XXXI

And I cried these words in the English tongue,
    " I am Peter Warbeckke,
From Katherine de Faro I am sprung
    And my father was John Osbeckke.

XXXII

" My father toiled and weaved with his hand,
    And bare neither sword nor shield;
And the White Rose of fair England
    Turned red on Bosworth field."

PERKIN WARBECK

XXXIII

And they gave me my life, but they held me fast
    Within this weary place;
But I wrought on my guards ere a month was past,
    With my wit and my comely face.

XXXIV

And they were ready to set me free,
    But when it was almost done,
And I thought I should gain the narrow sea
    And look on the face of the sun,

XXXV

The lord of the tower had word of it,
    And, alas! for my poor hope,
For this is the end of my face and my wit
    That to-morrow I die by the rope.

55

XXXVI

And the time draws nigh and the darkness closes,
  And the night is almost done.
What had I to do with their roses,
  I, the poor weaver's son ?

XXXVII

They promised me a bed so rich
  And a queen to be my bride,
And I have gotten a narrow ditch
  And a stake to pierce my side.

XXXVIII

They promised me a kingly part
  And a crown my head to deck,
And I have gotten the hangman's cart
  And a hempen cord for my neck.

PERKIN WARBECK

XXXIX

Oh! I would that I had never been born,
  To splendour and shame and sorrow,
For it's ill riding to grim Tiborne,
  Where I must ride to-morrow.

XL

I shall dress me all in silk and scarlet,
  And the hangman shall have my ring,
For though I be hanged like a low-born varlet
  They shall know I was once a king

XLI

And may I not fall faint or sick
  Till I reach at last to the goal,
And I pray that the rope may choke me quick
  And Christ receive my soul.

57

THE GARDEN OF DEATH

THERE is an isle in an unfurrowed sea
That I wot of, whereon the whole year round
The apple-blossoms and the rosebuds be
In early blooming ; and a many sound
Of ten-stringed lute, and most mellifluous breath
Of silver flute, and mellow half-heard horn,
Making unmeasured music.˙ Thither Death ˙
Coming like Love, takes all things in the morn
Of tenderest life, and being a delicate god,
In his own garden takes each delicate thing
Unstained, unmellowed, immature, untrod,
Tremulous betwixt the summer and the spring :
The rosebud ere it come to be a rose,
The blossom ere it win to be a fruit,

THE GARDEN OF DEATH

The virginal snowdrop, and the dove that knows
Only one dove for lover; all the loot
Of young soft things, and all the harvesting
Of unripe flowers.   Never comes the moon
To matron fulness, here no child-bearing
Vexes desire, and the sun knows no noon.
But all the happy dwellers of that place
Are reckless children, gotten on Delight
By Beauty that is thrall to Death; no grace,
No natural sweet they lack, a chrysolite
Of perfect beauty each.   No wisdom comes
To mar their early folly, no false laws
Man-made for man, no mouthing prudence numbs
Their green unthought, or gives their licence pause;
Young animals, young flowers, they live and grow,
And die before their sweet emblossomed breath
Has learnt to sigh save like a lover's.   Oh!
How sweet is Youth, how delicate is Death!

THE SPHINX

I GAZE across the Nile; flamelike and red
The sun goes down, and all the western sky
Is drowned in sombre crimson; wearily
A great bird flaps along with wings of lead,
Black on the rose-red river. Over my head
The sky is hard green bronze, beneath me lie
The sleeping ships; there is no sound, or sigh
Of the wind's breath,—a stillness of the dead.

Over a palm tree's top I see the peaks
Of the tall pyramids; and though my eyes
Are barred from it, I know that on the sand
Crouches a thing of stone that in some wise
Broods on my heart; and from the darkening land
Creeps Fear and to my soul in whisper speaks.

TO SHAKESPEARE

Most tuneful singer, lover tenderest,
Most sad, most piteous, and most musical,
Thine is the shrine more pilgrim-worn than all
The shrines of singers ; high above the rest
Thy trumpet sounds most loud, most manifest.
Yet better were it if a lonely call
Of woodland birds, a song, a madrigal,
Were all the jetsam of thy sea's unrest.

For now thy praises have become too loud
On vulgar lips, and every yelping cur
Yaps thee a pæan ; the whiles little men,
Not tall enough to worship in a crowd,
Spit their small wits at thee.   Ah! better then
The broken shrine, the lonely worshipper.

A SUMMER STORM

ALAS! how frail and weak a little boat
I have sailed in.   I called it Happiness,
And I had thought there was not storm nor stress
Of wind so masterful but it would float
Blithely in their despite ; but lo! one note
Of harsh discord, one word of bitterness,
And a fierce overwhelming wilderness
Of angry waters chokes my gasping throat.

I am near drowned in this unhappy sea,
I will not strive, let me lie still and sink,
I have no joy to live.   Oh! unkind love!
Why have you wounded me so bitterly ?
That am as easily wounded as a dove
Who has a silver throat and feet of pink.

AMORIS VINCULA

As a white dove that, in a cage of gold,
  Is prisoned from the air, and yet more bound
By love than bars, and will not wings unfold
  To fly away, though every gate be found
Unlocked and open; so my heart was caught,
  And linked to thine with triple links of love
But soon, a dove grown wanton, false it sought
  To break its chain, and faithless quite to rove
Where thou wouldst not; and with a painted bird
  Fluttered far off.   But when a moon was past,
Grown sick with longing for a voice unheard
  And lips unkissed, spread wings and home flew
    fast.
And lo! what seemed a sword to cleave its chain,
  Was but a link to rivet it again.

IN SARUM CLOSE

Tired of passion and the love that brings
Satiety's unrest, and failing sands
Of life, I thought to cool my burning hands
In this calm twilight of gray Gothic things:
But Love has laughed, and, spreading swifter wings
Than my poor pinions, once again with bands
Of silken strength my fainting heart commands,
And once again he plays on passionate strings.

But thou, my love, my flower, my jewel, set
In a fair setting, help me, or I die
To bear Love's burden; for that load to share
Is sweet and pleasant, but if lonely I
Must love unloved, 'tis pain; shine we, my fair
Two neighbour jewels in Love's coronet.

IMPRESSION DE NUIT

London

SEE what a mass of gems the city wears
Upon her broad live bosom! row on row
Rubies and emeralds and amethysts glow.
See! that huge circle like a necklace, stares
With thousands of bold eyes to heaven, and dares
The golden stars to dim the lamps below,
And in the mirror of the mire I know
The moon has left her image unawares.

That's the great town at night: I see her breasts,
Pricked out with lamps they stand like huge black
    towers,
I think they move! I hear her panting breath.
And that's her head where the tiara rests.
And in her brain, through lanes as dark as death,
Men creep like thoughts . . . The lamps are like
    pale flowers.

A SONG

STEAL from the meadows, rob the tall green hills,
  Ravish my orchard's blossoms, let me bind
A crown of orchard flowers and daffodils.
  Because my love is fair and white and kind.

To-day the thrush has trilled her daintiest phrases,
  Flowers with their incense have made drunk
    the air,
God has bent down to gild the hearts of daisies,
  Because my love is kind and white and fair.

To-day the sun has kissed the rose-tree's daughter,
  And sad Narcissus, Spring's pale acolyte
Hangs down his head and smiles into the water,
  Because my love is kind and fair and white

TO L——

Thou that wast once my loved and loving friend,
A friend no more, I had forgot thee quite,
Why hast thou come to trouble my delight .
With memories?   Oh! I had clean made end
Of all that time, I had made haste to send
My soul into red places, and to light
A torch of pleasure to burn up my night.
What I have woven hast thou come to rend?

In silent acres of forgetful flowers,
Crowned as of old with happy daffodils,
Long time my wounded soul has been a-straying,
Alas! it has chanced now on sombre hours
Of hard remembrances and sad delaying,
Leaving green valleys for the bitter hills.

IN WINTER

Oh! for a day of burning noon
  And a sun like a glowing ember,
Oh! for one hour of golden June,
  In the heart of this chill November.

I can scarcely remember the Spring's soft breath,
  Or imagine the Summer hazes :
The yellow woods are so damp with death
  That I have forgotten the daisies.

68

IN WINTER

Oh! to lie watching the sky again,
From a nest of hot grass and clover,
Till the stars come out like golden rain
When the lazy day is over,

And crowning the night with an aureole,
As the clouds kiss and drift asunder,
The moon floats up like a luminous soul,
And the stars grow pale for wonder.

PLAINTE ETERNELLE

THE sun sinks down, the tremulous daylight dies.
　(Down their long shafts the weary sunbeams
　　glide.)
　The white-winged ships drift with the falling
　　tide,
Come back, my love, with pity in your eyes!

The tall white ships drift with the falling tide.
　(Far, far away I hear the seamews' cries.)
　Come back, my love, with pity in your eyes!
There is no room now in my heart for pride.

PLAINTE ETERNELLE

Come back, come back! with pity in your eyes.
   (The night is dark, the sea is fierce and wide.)
   There is no room now in my heart for pride,
Though I become the scorn of all the wise.

I have no place now in my heart for pride.
   (The moon and stars have fallen from the skies.)
   Though I become the scorn of all the wise,
Thrust, if you will, sharp arrows in my side.

Let me become the scorn of all the wise.
   (Out of the East I see the morning ride.)
   Thrust, if you will, sharp arrows in my side,
Play with my tears and feed upon my sighs.

Wound me with swords, put arrows in my side.
   (On the white sea the haze of noon-day lies.)
   Play with my tears and feed upon my sighs,
But come, my love, before my heart has died.

PLAINTE ETERNELLE

Drink my salt tears and feed upon my sighs.
  (Westward the evening goes with one red stride.)
  Come back, my love, before my heart has died,
Down sinks the sun, the tremulous daylight dies.

Come back! my love, before my heart has died.
  (Out of the South I see the pale moon rise.)
  Down sinks the sun, the tremulous daylight dies,
The white-winged ships drift with the falling tide.

IN SUMMER

THERE were the black pine trees,
  And the sullen hills
  Frowning; there were trills
  Of birds, and the sweet hot sun,
  And little rills
  Of water, everyone
Singing and prattling; there were bees

Honey-laden, tuneful, a song
  Far-off, and a timid air
  That sighed and kissed my hair,
  My hair that the hot sun loves.
  The day was very fair,

IN SUMMER

There was wooing of doves,
And the shadows were not yet long.

And I lay on the soft green grass,
        And the smell of the earth was sweet,
        And I dipped my feet
        In the little stream ;
        And was cool as a flower is cool in the heat,
        And the day lay still in a dream,
And the hours forgot to pass.

And you came, my love, so stealthily
        That I saw you not
        Till I felt that your arms were hot
        Round my neck, and my lips were wet
        With your lips, I had forgot
        How sweet you were.   And lo ! the sun
            had set,
And the pale moon came up silently.

NIGHT COMING INTO A GARDEN

Roses red and white,
  Every rose is hanging her head,
Silently comes the lady Night,
  Only the flowers can hear her tread.

All day long the birds have been calling,
  Calling shrill and sweet,
They are still when she comes with her long robe
      falling,
  Falling down to her feet.

NIGHT COMING INTO A GARDEN

The thrush has sung to his mate,
  "She is coming! hush! she is coming!"
She is lifting the latch at the gate,
  And the bees have ceased from their humming.

I cannot see her face as she passes
  Through my garden of white and red;
But I know she has walked where the daisies and
    grasses
  Are curtseying after her tread.

She has passed me by with a rustle and sweep
  Of her robe (as she passed I heard it sweeping),
And all my red roses have fallen asleep,
  And all my white roses are sleeping.

NIGHT GOING OUT OF A GARDEN

Through the still air of night

 Suddenly comes, alone and shrill,

Like the far-off voice of the distant light,

 The single piping trill

Of a bird that has caught the scent of the dawn,

 And knows that the night is over;

(She has poured her dews on the velvet lawn

 And drenched the long grass and the clover,)

And now with her naked white feet

 She is silently passing away,

Out of the garden and into the street,

Over the long yellow fields of the wheat,

  Till she melts in the arms of the day.

And from the great gates of the East,

  With a clang and a brazen blare,

Forth from the rosy wine and the feast

  Comes the god with the flame-flaked hair;

The hoofs of his horses ring

  On the golden stones, and the wheels

Of his chariot burn and sing,

  And the earth beneath him reels;

And forth with a rush and a rout

  His myriad angels run,

And the world is awake with a shout,

  " He is coming! The sun! The sun!"

JONQUIL AND FLEUR-DE-LYS

I

Jonquil was a shepherd lad,
  White he was as the curded cream,
Hair like the buttercups he had,
  And wet green eyes like a full chalk stream.

II

His teeth were as white as the stones that lie
  Down in the depths of the sun-bright river,
And his lashes danced like a dragon-fly
  With drops on the gauzy wings that quiver.

III

His lips were as red as round ripe cherries,
  And his delicate cheeks and his rose-pink neck,
Were stained with the colour of dog-rose berries
  When they lie on the snow like a crimson fleck.

IV

His feet were all stained with the cowslips and
  grass
  To amber and verdigris,
And through his folds one day did pass
  The young prince Fleur-de-lys.

V

Fleur-de-lys was the son of the king.
  He was as white as an onyx stone,
His hair was curled like a daffodil ring,
  And his eyes were like gems in the queen's blue
  zone.

VI

His teeth were as white as the white pearls set
  Round the thick white throat of the queen in
    the hall,
And his lashes were like the dark silk net
  That she binds her yellow hair withal.

VII

His lips were as red as the red rubies
  The king's bright dagger-hilt that deck,
And pale rose-pink as the amethyst is
  Were his delicate cheeks and his rose-pink neck.

VIII

His feet were all shod in shoes of gold,
  And his coat was as gold as a blackbird's bill is,
With jewel on jewel manifold,
  And wrought with a pattern of golden lilies.

G   81

IX

When Fleur-de-lys espied Jonquil
  He was as glad as a bird in May ;
He tripped right swiftly a-down the hill,
  And called to the shepherd boy to play.

X

This fell out ere the sheep-shearing,
  That these two lads did sport and toy
Fleur-de-lys the son of the king,
  And sweet Jonquil the shepherd boy

XI

And after they had played awhile,
  Thereafter they to talking fell,
And full an hour they did beguile
  While each his state and lot did tell.

XII

For Jonquil spake of the little sheep,
 And the tender ewes that know their names,
And he spake of his wattled hut for sleep,
 And the country sports and the shepherds'
  games.

XIII

And he plucked a reed from the edge that girds
 The river bank, and with his knife
Made a pipe, with a breath like the singing birds
 When they flute to their loves in a musical strife.

XIV

And he told of the night so long and still
 When he lay awake till he heard the feet
Of the goat-foot god coming over the hill,
 And the rustling sound as he passed through
  the wheat.

JONQUIL AND FLEUR-DE-LŸS

XV

And Fleur-de-lys told of the king and the court,
  And the stately dames and the slender pages,
Of his horse and his hawk and his mimic fort, ⁚
  And the silent birds in their golden cages.

XVI

And the jewelled sword with the damask blade
  That should be his in his fifteenth spring;
And the silver sound that the gold horns made,
  And the tourney lists and the tilting ring.

XVII

And after that they did devise
  For mirth and sport, that each should wear
The other's clothes, and in this guise
  Make play each other's parts to bear.

JONQUIL AND FLEUR-DE-LYS

XVIII.

Whereon they stripped off all their clothes,
    And when they stood up in the sun,
They were as like as one white rose
    On one green stalk, to another one.

XIX

And when Jonquil as a prince was shown
    And Fleur-de-lys as a shepherd lad,
Their mothers' selves would not have known
    That each the other's habit had.

XX

And Jonquil walked like the son of a king
    With dainty steps and high haut look;
And Fleur-de-lys, that sweet youngling,
    Did push and paddle his feet in the brook.

XXI

And while they made play in this wise,
  Unto them all in haste did run,
Two lords of the court, with joyful cries,
  That long had sought the young king's son.

XXII

And to Jonquil they reverence made
  And said, " My lord, we are come from the king,
Who is sore vexed that thou hast strayed
  So far without a following."

XXIII

Then unto them said Fleur-de-lys
  " You do mistake, my lords, for know
That I am the son of the king, and this
  Is sweet Jonquil, my playfellow."

XXIV

Whereat one of these lords replied,
  " Thou lying knave, I'll make thee rue
Such saucy words."   But Jonquil cried,
  " Nay, nay, my lord, 'tis even true."

XXV

Whereat these lords were sore distressed,
  And one made answer bending knee,
" My lord the prince is pleased to jest."
  But Jonquil answered, " Thou shalt see.

XXVI

" Sure never yet so strange a thing
  As this before was seen,
That a shepherd was thought the son of a king,
  And a prince a shepherd boy to have been.

XXVII

" Now mark me well, my noble lord,
    A shepherd's feet go bare and cold,
Therefore they are all green from the sward,
    And the buttercup makes a stain of gold.

XXVIII

" That I am Jonquil thus shalt thou know,
    And that this be very Fleur-de-lys
If his feet be like the driven snow,
    And mine like the amber and verdigris."

XXIX

He lifted up the shepherd's frock
    That clothed the prince, and straight did show
That his naked feet all under his smock
    Were whiter than the driven snow.

88

JONQUIL AND FLEUR-DE-LYS

XXX

He doffed the shoes and the clothes of silk
  That he had gotten from Fleur-de-lys,
And all the rest was as white as milk,
  But his feet were like amber and verdigris.

XXXI

With that they each took back his own,
  And when this second change was done,
As a shepherd boy was Jonquil shown
  And Fleur-de-lys the king's true son.

XXXII

By this the sun was low in the heaven,
  And Fleur-de-lys must ride away,
But ere he left, with kisses seven,
  He vowed to come another day.

89

A WINTER SUNSET

The frosty sky, like a furnace burning,
   The keen air, crisp and cold,
   And a sunset that splashes the clouds with
      gold ;
But my heart to summer turning.

Come back, sweet summer ! come back again !
   I hate the snow,
   And the icy winds that the north lands blow,
And the fall of the frozen rain.

A WINTER SUNSET

I hate the iron ground,
    And the Christmas roses,
    And the sickly day that dies when it closes,
With never a song or a sound.

Come back! come back! with your passionate heat
    And glowing hazes,
    And your sun that shines as a lover gazes,
And your day with the tired feet.

APOLOGIA

TELL me not of Philosophies,

Of morals, ethics, laws of life ;

Give me no subtle theories,

No instruments of wordy strife.

I will not forge laborious chains

Link after link, till seven times seven,

I need no ponderous iron cranes

To haul my soul from earth to heaven.

But with a burnished wing,

Rainbow-hued in the sun,

I will dive and leap and run

APOLOGIA

In the air, and I will bring
Back to the earth a heavenly thing.
  I will dance through the stars
  And pass the blue bars
Of heaven.   I will catch hands with God
  And speak with him,
  I will kiss the lips of the seraphim
  And the deep-eyed cherubim;
I will pluck of the flowers that nod
  Row upon row upon row,
In the infinite gardens of God,
To the breath of the wind of the sweep of the
      lyres,
  And the cry of the strings
  And the golden wires,
  And the mystical musical things
That the world may not know.

IN MEMORIAM

(D)

Oct. 18, 1894

DEAR friend, dear brother, I have owed you this
Since many days, the tribute of a song.
Shall I cheat you who never did a wrong
To any man? No, therefore though I miss
All art, all skill, in this short armistice
From my soul's war against the bitter throng
Of present woes, let these poor lines be strong
In love enough to bear a brother's kiss.

Dear saint, true knight, I cannot weep for you,
Nor if I could would I call back the breath
To your dear body; God is very wise,
All that this year had in its womb He knew,
And, loving you, He sent His son like Death,
To put His hand over your kind gray eyes.

A PRAYER

Often the western wind has sung to me,
There have been voices in the streams and meres,
And pitiful trees have told me, God, of Thee:
And I heard not.   Oh! open Thou mine ears.

The reeds have whispered low as I passed by,
" Be strong, O friend, be strong, put off vain fears,
Vex not thy soul with doubts, God cannot lie:"
And I heard not.   Oh! open Thou mine ears.

95

A PRAYER

There have been many stars to guide my feet,
Often the delicate moon, hearing my sighs,
Has rent the clouds and shown a silver street;
And I saw not.   Oh! open Thou mine eyes.

Angels have beckoned me unceasingly,
And walked with me; and from the sombre skies
Dear Christ Himself has stretched out hands to me;
And I saw not.   Oh! open Thou mine eyes.

AUTUMN DAYS

I HAVE been through the woods to-day,
  And the leaves were falling,
Summer had crept away,
  And the birds were not calling.

And the bracken was like yellow gold
  That comes too late,
When the heart is sad and old,
  And death at the gate.

AUTUMN DAYS

Ah, mournful Autumn! Sad,
  Slow death that comes at last,
I am mad for a yesterday, mad!
  I am sick for a year that is past!

Though the sun be like blood in the sky
  He is cold as the lips of hate,
And he fires the sere leaves as they lie
  On their bed of earth, too late.

They are dead, and the bare trees weep
  Not loud as a mortal weeping,
But as sorrow that sighs in sleep,
  And as grief that is still in sleeping.

THE IMAGE OF DEATH

I CARVED an image coloured like the night,
Winged with huge wings, stern-browed and men-
 acing,
With hair caught back, and diademed like a king :
The left hand held a sceptre, and the right
Grasped a sharp sword, the bitter marble lips
Were curled and proud ; the yellow topaz eyes
(Each eye a jewel) stared in fearful wise ;
The hard fierce limbs were bare, and from the hips
A scourge hung down.   And on the pedestal
I wrote these words, " O all things that have breath,

THE IMAGE OF DEATH

This is the image of the great god Death,
Pour ye the wine and bind the coronal!
Pipe unto him with pipes and flute with flutes,
Woo him with flowers and spices odorous,
Let singing boys with lips mellifluous
Make madrigals and lull his ear with lutes.
Anon bring sighs and tears of harsh distress,
And weeping wounds! so haply ye may move
A heart of stone, from breasts of hate suck love,
Or garner pity from the pitiless."

TO SLEEP

Ah, Sleep, to me thou com'st not in the guise
Of one who brings good gifts to weary men,
Balm for bruised hearts and fancies alien
To unkind truth, and drying for sad eyes.
I dread the summons to that fierce assize
Of all my foes and woes, that waits me when
Thou makest my soul the unwilling denizen
Of thy dim troubled house where unrest lies.

My soul is sick with dreaming, let it rest.
False Sleep, thou hast conspired with Wakefulness,
I will not praise thee, I too long beguiled
With idle tales.   Where is thy soothing breast?
Thy peace, thy poppies, thy forgetfulness?
Where is thy lap for me so tired a child?

VÆ VICTIS!

HERE in this isle

The summer still lingers,

And Autumn's brown fingers

So busy the while

With the leaves in the north,

Are scarcely put forth

In this land where the sun still glows like an

ember,

In mid-November.

VÆ VICTIS

In England it's cold,
And the yellow and red
Of October have fled;
    And the sun is wet gold
    Like an emperor weeping,
When Death goes a-reaping
All through his empire, merciless comer,
    The dead things of summer.

The sky has cried so
That the earth is all sodden,
With dead leaves in-trodden,
    And the trees to and fro
    Wave their arms in the air
    In despair, in despair:
They are thinking of all the hot days that are
        over,
    And the cows in the clover.

VÆ VICTIS

Here the roses are out,
And the sun at high noon
Makes the birds faint and swoon.

But the cricket's about
With his song, and the hum
Of the bees as they come
To feast at the honey-board laden and groaning,
Makes musical droning.

But vainly, alas!
Do I hide in the south,
Kiss close with my mouth
Red flowers, green grass,
For Autumn has found me
And thrown her arms round me.
She has breathed on my lips and I wander apart,
Dead leaves in my heart.

Capri.

REJECTED

ALAS! I have lost my God,
  My beautiful God Apollo.
Wherever his footsteps trod
  My feet were wont to follow.

But oh! it fell out one day
  My soul was so heavy with weeping,
That I laid me down by the way;
  And he left me while I was sleeping.

REJECTED

And my soul awoke in the night,
  And I bowed my ear for his fluting,
And I heard but the breath of the flight
  Of wings and the night-birds hooting.

And night drank all her cup,
  And I went to the shrine in the hollow,
And the voice of my cry went up:
  "Apollo! Apollo! Apollo!"

But he never came to the gate,
  And the sun was hid in a mist,
And there came one walking late,
  And I knew it was Christ.

He took my soul and bound it
  With cords of iron wire,
Seven times round He wound it
  With the cords of my desire.

REJECTED

The cords of my desire,
　While my desire slept,
Were seven bands of wire
　To bind my soul that wept.

And He hid my soul at last
　In a place of stones and fears,
Where the hours like days went past
　And the days went by like years.

And after many days
　That which had slept awoke,
And desire burnt in a blaze,
　And my soul went up in the smoke

And we crept away from the place
　And would not look behind,
And the angel that hides his face
　Was crouched on the neck of the wind.

REJECTED

And I went to the shrine in the hollow
  Where the lutes and the flutes were playing,
And I cried: " I am come, Apollo,
  Back to thy shrine, from my straying."

But he would have none of my soul
  That was stained with blood and with tears,
That had lain in the earth like a mole,
  In the place of great stones and fears.

And now I am lost in the mist
  Of the things that can never be,
For I will have none of Christ
  And Apollo will none of me.

ODE TO MY SOUL

RISE up my soul!
Shake thyself from the dust.
Lift up thy head that wears an aureole,
Fulfil thy trust.
Out of the mire where they would trample thee
Make images of clay,
Whereon having breathed, from thy divinity
Let them take mighty wings and soar away
    Right up to God.
Out of thy broken past
Where impious feet have trod,

ODE TO MY SOUL

Build thee a golden house august and vast,

Whereto these worms of earth may some day crawl.

Let there be nothing small

Henceforth with thee ;

Take thou unbounded scorn of all their scorn,

    Eternity

Of high contempt : be thou no more forlorn

But proud in thy immortal loneliness,

And infinite distress :

And, being 'mid mortal things divinely born,

Rise up my soul !

Printed by R. & R. CLARK, LIMITED, *Edinburgh*

SELECTED LIST OF
MR. GRANT RICHARDS'S PUBLICATIONS
IN BELLES-LETTRES

A SHROPSHIRE LAD. By A. E. HOUSMAN. Fcap. 8vo, buckram, 3s. 6d. net.

THE WIND IN THE TREES : A Book of Country Verse. By KATHERINE TYNAN (Mrs. Hinkson). Fcap. 8vo, cloth, 3s. 6d. net.

'ENGLAND AND YESTERDAY': A Book of Short Poems. By LOUISE IMOGEN GUINEY. Royal 16mo, cloth.

SPIKENARD : A Book of Devotional Love Poems. By LAURENCE HOUSMAN. With Cover designed by the Author. Small 4to, boards, 3s. 6d. net.

PORPHYRION, and Other Poems. By LAURENCE BINYON. Crown 8vo, buckram, 5s. net.

HAFIZ : Versions from the Divan of. By WALTER LEAF, LL.D. Post 4to, 5s. net.

OMAR KHAYYÁM, RUBÁIYAT OF : A Paraphrase. By RICHARD LE GALLIENNE. Long fcap. 8vo, parchment cover, 5s. net.

⁎ A 'Breviary' Edition, limited to 1000 copies for sale, is also issued. 18mo, green calf, 8s. net.

REALMS OF UNKNOWN KINGS. By LAURENCE ALMA-TADEMA. Fcap. 8vo, buckram, 3s. net. Paper covers, 2s. net.

AGLAVAINE AND SELYSETTE: A Drama in Five
Acts. By MAURICE MAETERLINCK. Translated by
ALFRED SUTRO. With an Introduction by W. J.
MACKAIL, and Title-page designed by W. H. MARGET-
SON. Globe 8vo, half buckram, 2s. 6d. net.

THE INFERNO. By DANTE. Translated into English
Verse by EUGENE LEE-HAMILTON. Fcap. 8vo, half
parchment, 3s. net.

PLAYS: PLEASANT AND UNPLEASANT. By G.
BERNARD SHAW. With a portrait of the Author in
photogravure. 2 vols. Fcap. 8vo, 10s.

A BOOK OF VERSES FOR CHILDREN. By EDWARD
VERRALL LUCAS. With Cover, Title-page, and End-
Papers designed in colours by F. D. BEDFORD. Crown
8vo, 6s.

THE FLOWER OF THE MIND. By ALICE MEYNELL.
A Choice among the best Poems. With Cover designed
by LAURENCE HOUSMAN. Crown 8vo, buckram, 6s.

, 250 copies have also been bound in Japanese parchment,
with silk ties, 7s. 6d. net.

LIMBO, and other Essays. By VERNON LEE. With
Frontispiece. Fcap. 8vo, buckram, 5s. net.

LONDON IN SONG: An Anthology of Prose and Poetry
inspired by London. By WILFRED WHITTEN. With an
Introduction. With Cover, Title-page, and End-papers
designed in colours by WILLIAM HYDE. Crown 8vo, 6s.

THE FIELD FLORIDUS, and Other Poems. By EUGENE
MASON. Fcap. 8vo, half parchment, 5s. net.

———————

LONDON
GRANT RICHARDS
9 HENRIETTA STREET, COVENT GARDEN, W.C.